DC COMICS

SUPER HEROES

D0491874

FRIENDS AND FOES!

BY TREY KING   ILLUSTRATED BY SEAN WANG

■SCHOLASTIC

SCHOLASTIC CHILDREN'S BOOKS
EUSTON HOUSE,
24 EVERSHOLT STREET,
LONDON NW1 1DB, UK

A DIVISION OF SCHOLASTIC LTD
LONDON ~ NEW YORK ~ TORONTO ~ SYDNEY ~ AUCKLAND
MEXICO CITY ~ NEW DELHI ~ HONG KONG

THIS BOOK WAS FIRST PUBLISHED IN THE US IN 2015 BY SCHOLASTIC INC.
PUBLISHED IN THE UK BY SCHOLASTIC LTD, 2016

ISBN 978 1407 16264 5

PRINTED AND BOUND IN ITALY

2 4 6 8 10 9 7 5 3 1

PAPERS USED BY SCHOLASTIC CHILDREN'S BOOKS ARE MADE FROM
WOODS GROWN IN SUSTAINABLE FORESTS.

WWW.SCHOLASTIC.CO.UK

"YOU DON'T HAVE TO HANDLE IT ALONE," SAYS SUPERMAN.
"THAT'S WHAT FRIENDS ARE FOR!" SAYS WONDER WOMAN.
"BATMAN AND I AREN'T REALLY FRIENDS. HE'S MORE LIKE MY BOSS," SAYS BATGIRL, "BUT I CAN HELP, TOO."

BATMAN AND SUPERMAN START TO ARGUE. THEY ARE BEST FRIENDS, BUT SOMETIMES THEY DISAGREE ABOUT HOW TO SAVE THE DAY.

"DO THEY ALWAYS DO THIS?" BATGIRL ASKS.
"ALL THE TIME," SAYS WONDER WOMAN.

SUPERMAN AND BATMAN TAKE TO THE SKY IN A RACE TO FIND THE SUPER-VILLAINS. THE JOKER IS A DANGEROUS CLOWN, AND DARKSEID IS AN ALIEN THREAT FROM OUTER SPACE! BUT WHERE COULD THEY BE?

WHILE THEY'RE DISTRACTED, DARKSEID SHOOTS A BEAM OF RED ENERGY FROM HIS EYES AND ZAPS THE SUPER HEROES. THEY ARE KNOCKED OUT! "NOW, THAT'S FUNNY!" THE JOKER LAUGHS. "YOU SHOULD HAVE ATTACKED US BAD GUYS WHEN YOU HAD THE CHANCE, SILLY HEROES."

REALIZING HOW THEY GOT HERE, THE HEROES DECIDE TO MAKE THINGS RIGHT. "SORRY FOR THE WAY I ACTED," SAYS BATMAN. "I NEED TO LEARN HOW TO WORK BETTER AS PART OF A TEAM."

"I'M SORRY, TOO," SAYS SUPERMAN. "I GUESS I SHOULD LEARN TO SHARE THE VILLAINS."